for Heat
Lanse Isaacson

W9-CRO-839

DATE DUE

MAR 2 0	ACH		
MTE	JAN 2 0		

DEMCO 38-296

ALISON GOES FOR THE GOLD
by Catherine Connor

Illustrations by
Gabriel Picart

Spot Illustrations by
Rich Grote

MagicAtt c
Club

MAGIC ATTIC PRESS

Published by Magic Attic Press.

For more information contact:
Book Editor, Magic Attic Press, 866 Spring Street,
P.O. Box 9712, Portland, ME 04104-9954

First Edition
Printed in the United States of America
1 2 3 4 5 6 7 8 9 10

Betsy Gould, Editorial Director
Marva Martin, Art Director
Robin Haywood, Managing Editor

Edited by Judit Bodnar
Designed by Susi Oberhelman

Library of Congress Cataloging-in-Publications Data

ISBN: 1-57513-002-5

CIP 95-77944

As members of the
MAGIC ATTIC CLUB,
we promise to
be best friends,
share all of our adventures in the attic,
use our imaginations,
have lots of fun together,
and remember—the real magic is in us.

Alison   *Keisha*

Heather   *Megan*

Table of Contents

Chapter

One

A NEW CHALLENGE

esss!" said Keisha Vance, punching the air with her thumb.

"Way to go, Ali!" Heather Hardin whispered.

Alison McCann smiled proudly as Ms. Austin finished her announcement to the class. "And so, the runoff election for class president, between Alison McCann and Brittany Foster, will take place Monday morning."

Megan Ryder reached across the aisle to pat Ali's shoulder. "I told you you'd be nominated," she said.

Just as Ms. Austin finished her announcement, the recess bell clanged. As the kids lined up to go to the playground, Noah Cummings patted Alison's arm.

"Congratulations, President McCann!" he said. "Sounds good to me."

"Right on," said Ben Benchley, with a grin.

"Thanks, you guys," Alison said, suddenly feeling bashful. She wondered if she should ask Noah and Ben for their votes the way a real politician would, but she was afraid they might think she was too self-centered or something. So she said nothing. The problem is, she thought, I don't know how to get the kids to vote for me without sounding too full of myself.

That question stayed in Alison's mind all day, but she didn't come up with an answer until she'd finished her homework that afternoon. She thought of what her three friends had said. They'd suggested that she think of things she could do to make kids vote for her, to try to think the way the other kids in the class would. What would make me want one person to win instead of another? Alison asked herself. I'd like to know that the class president wanted to make my life in school better, make it more interesting. And the only way to find out what the kids want is to ask.

Without wasting a minute, she turned to her computer

and began to write out a questionnaire. She asked things like what the kids thought of school, what changes they would like made in class and how she could improve student spirit. In the morning, Alison, Keisha, and Heather helped hand out the questionnaires, talking to every student in her grade and asking each one to fill out the forms and give them to Alison the following morning.

After school on Wednesday, the four friends went straight to Alison's house and read all the answers before they went home. As soon as she finished supper, Alison sat down at her computer and began to type up her platform. First she eliminated suggestions like improving the cafeteria menu by getting rid of gray peas and finding out the contents of the weekly mystery meat. Then she wrote out seven campaign promises, with explanations of how she would accomplish each of her goals.

"Good job!" said Ali's thirteen-year-old brother, Mark, when she showed him the list. "Looks like you're living up to the McCann motto: Play hard, play to win." Alison smiled proudly, hoping her father would also approve of her winning strategy. So far, she had managed to live up to the family expectations. She made good grades and was an outstanding athlete, always working hard to accomplish her goals. She was surprised to be nominated for class president, though.

She intended to give a copy of her campaign
promises to every kid in the class so they'd all know what
she stood for. But the moment Alison, Keisha, Heather,
and Megan arrived at school on Thursday morning, they
were confronted by a huge photograph of Brittany glued
on a pink and blue campaign poster that was taped
on the wall next to the classroom door. Brittany's smiling
image looked straight into the camera as she pointed her
finger. The caption underneath read: "Brittany Foster
Wants Your Vote."

Alison stopped in her tracks. When she glanced at the
ordinary-looking campaign promises in her hand, her
heart sank.

Heather put her arm around Alison's shoulder and
said, "You know, the kids are really going to be impressed
with your ideas for making school life more interesting."

Alison nodded. "Sure they are. . . ."

Standing beside Alison, Megan inspected the poster
carefully. "That poster's not such a big deal," she finally said.

"Brittany looks like a movie star," Alison said.

"Too bad it's not Freddie Kreuger," Keisha mumbled.

At first, Alison managed to shrug off Brittany's poster.
Then she saw more posters in the girl's bathroom, the
auditorium, and the cafeteria. This could mean trouble,
Alison thought. Big trouble. That's when she asked

Heather and Megan and Keisha, "If our parents will let us spend the night together, do you think you could help me make posters this evening?"

After promising to do their homework and go to bed on time, the girls got special permission for a sleepover, even though it was a school night. As soon as they finished dinner, they gathered in Alison's bedroom and got to work.

"What do you think?" Alison leaned against her blue and white flowered bedspread and held up the poster she was working on. Bottles of silver glitter and a pile of magic markers lay scattered on the floor next to her. "The combination of my campaign promises and this poster should really wow the class."

Heather studied the poster. "I think it needs more butterflies," she said, pushing her long, dark hair out of her eyes. "The brighter the better—red and blue and yellow. Primary colors attract attention."

Keisha laughed. "Now you know why I wear bright colors," she said.

Megan inspected the artwork silently. The border was decorated with rainbows, butterflies, and daisies. Inside, Alison had printed:

VOTE FOR THE CANDIDATE WHO
CARES ABOUT YOU!
ALISON McCANN FOR PRESIDENT

"I think," said Megan thoughtfully, "you should print *Alison McCann for President* in larger letters on the next one."

"And I think you should outline all the lettering with gold," said Keisha.

Heather's eyes lit up. "Gold? Great idea!" she said. "Then you could match it by putting a golden key in each corner. We'd be the only ones to know that they stand for the Magic Attic Club. It would be our secret."

Alison smiled. She loved spending the night with her three best friends. She and Megan and Keisha had known each other since kindergarten. Even though Heather had moved to town only a few months ago, she immediately fit in with the other three friends. "The

Musketeers of Primrose Street," Alison's mother called them. "All for one and one for all."

But the connection between the girls went beyond their neighborhood friendship. In the attic of their neighbor, Ellie Goodwin, they could choose any costume they wished from Ellie's large antique trunk. Each time they tried on an outfit in front of the mirror, they were carried away to a different time and place. Everything that happened in the attic seemed magical, and the Magic Attic Club was their special secret. The four girls shared each new and exciting adventure.

Now they were sharing a different kind of adventure: Alison's campaign for class president. In a way, a victory for Alison would be a victory for all of them.

The girls worked nonstop throughout the evening. By the time they went to bed that night, they had decorated twelve posters. Before class even started the next morning, they had already taped and tacked the glittering, colorful posters all over the school.

"That ought to do it," said Alison, stepping back to admire the poster she had just taped on the classroom door. She touched it for luck before going into class.

Alison started the morning in reading class, her least favorite subject. Reading had never been easy for her. Sometimes she got the words turned around in her head, so they were hard to understand. Other times she'd confuse words like *diary* and *dairy* or *trail* and *trial*. Even though Alison tried really hard, she didn't always see the difference. It made her feel foolish and frustrated.

Today she was especially eager to leave and see how the kids reacted to her posters. When the bell rang, she motioned to her friends and hurried out of the room.

"Stop!" cried Keisha as the girls hustled into the hallway. Alison, Megan, and Heather put on their brakes. "Look." Keisha pointed to the blank space beside the classroom door.

"What happened to my poster?" Alison asked, checking to see if it had fallen onto the floor. The poster was nowhere in sight.

The girls ran to the bathroom and the cafeteria, to the auditorium and the art room. Throughout the school, Brittany Foster's face stared at them. But every one of Alison's posters, every brilliant butterfly and glittering rainbow, every yellow daisy and golden key, had disappeared.

Chapter

Two

A DIFFERENT SOLUTION

Rachel Harmon ran to the far corner of the playground, where Alison stood with some of her friends. "Someone stole your posters!" she cried.

"I know," Alison said, with a frown. "What I don't understand is why anybody would do it."

Megan shrugged. "That's easy," she said. "They'd do it to win."

"I don't get it," Alison protested. "Winning means the kids think you're the best person for the job, so they vote for you."

"Earth to Ali, Earth to Ali. It doesn't exactly go that way," said Noah Cummings. "This election's no different than a game of tennis. The winner isn't the one who's the nicest. It's the one who scores the most points."

"But still . . ." Alison protested.

"But what?" said Rachel. "There are lots of people who will do anything to win."

"I know you have to try your best to beat the people you compete against," Alison replied. "I do it all the time in sports. It helps me play harder. But I wouldn't take someone's posters."

Shaking her head slowly, Heather asked, "Who's running for president against you?"

"Brittany," said Alison.

"Whose posters are still hanging all over the school?"

"Brittany's." Alison paused. "I admit that Brittany and I haven't ever been what I'd call good friends, but I didn't think she was the kind of person who'd take my posters."

"Look," said Keisha, "she wants to be president of the class. Do you *really* think she'd risk being caught stealing posters? That could ruin everything for her."

"I guess it depends on how much she wants to win," said Heather.

"Well, nobody in the world likes to win more than I do," Alison said with a laugh.

"Maybe," said Keisha, "but, like Rachel said, lots of people don't play by the rules."

"Then what do I do?" asked Alison.

"Sometimes you've got to fight fire with fire," said Rachel.

"What do you mean?" asked Alison.

"I think she means maybe some of Brittany's posters ought to meet with a fatal accident, too," Noah drawled.

"Yeah," said Heather.

"Right on," said Keisha.

Megan held up her hands. "Objection, objection," she said, mimicking her mother, who was an attorney. "As far

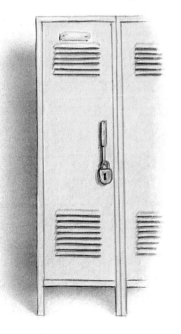

as I know, in this country you're innocent until proven guilty. And none of us knows if Brittany's the one who did this."

All six kids were silent as they entered the school building and walked down the hall to class. Then Alison gave a decisive nod. "You're right," she said. "We can't do anything till we're positive Brittany took my posters."

"I still think you should do *something*," Noah said.

"That's no problem," said Alison as she stopped in front of the classroom door. She reached into her pocket and pulled out a felt tip pen. "I wonder . . . I wonder how Brittany would look with a mustache," she said devilishly.

"You wouldn't!" gasped Heather.

"You shouldn't!" said Megan.

"A mustache would bring out the *green* in Brittany's eyes," Keisha said with a grin. "Don't you agree?"

Alison laughed, waving the pen in front of the poster and pretending to mark it up. "Take that!" she said, as if she were brandishing a sword. "And that! And that!"

Just then, the final bell rang. "Well," said Keisha, "if anyone doesn't deserve to be saved by the bell, it's Brittany Foster."

"Alison?" asked Ms. Austin as the kids entered the classroom.

Alison walked over to her teacher's desk. "Yes, Ma'am," she said.

"Alison, did you remove your campaign posters?"

Swallowing, Alison answered, "No."

"You mean someone else took them?"

Alison nodded, twirling the mustache pen in her fingers as she spoke.

"I see," said Ms. Austin thoughtfully.

On the way to her desk, Alison tried to catch Brittany's

eye, but her rival refused to look at her. Instead, Brittany giggled nervously and sat down across the aisle from Janie Kirkland, her best friend.

"Class," said Ms. Austin from the front of the room. She waited patiently until the students were silent. "It's come to my attention that Alison's campaign posters have been removed." As the teacher spoke, Brittany stared at her pencil as if it were a rare dinosaur bone recently discovered in Outer Mongolia. "Since the election is Monday, it would be foolish to ask Alison to spend her weekend making her posters over again. And so I'd like to ask you how you think we could rectify this problem."

For a moment, the class was silent. Then Maria Garfias raised her hand. "Maybe we could help Alison make some new posters," she suggested.

Ms. Austin nodded. "That's a good idea. Any others?"

Linda Chang suggested that Brittany should apologize to Alison, but Ms. Austin reminded the class that Brittany hadn't even been accused of any wrongdoing. Nathan Steiner said he thought the class should have another run-off election. "Why don't we ask Brittany to take down all her posters?" said Rachel Harmon. "Then everything would be even."

Brittany's hand shot up. "That's not fair!" she said. "It's Alison's problem that her posters were stolen!"

"I didn't say the posters were stolen," said Ms. Austin.

Brittany looked at her pencil again. "Oh."

"Actually," the teacher continued, "I'd like to ask Alison what she thinks."

Alison sighed. "It's hard," she said. "I don't want to punish anyone who doesn't deserve it. But . . ."

Ms. Austin nodded. "Go on."

"Well," said Alison, "even though Brittany's posters probably get more attention than the campaign promises I passed out, I think my ideas can hold their own. So, the way I see it, Brittany should be able to keep her posters as long as I know all the fifth graders have really read my platform. I want the kids to know that I'm serious about ideas like working to get more class trips and figuring out ways to raise money so we can buy more computers."

"That seems fair to me," said Ms. Austin. "Why don't we take five minutes right now so everyone can read Alison's platform. Over the weekend you can think about the platform and about Brittany's posters. Then Monday morning we'll have our election as scheduled. Do you think that sounds fair, class?"

Everyone nodded except Brittany.

"It looks like the majority supports that decision," Ms. Austin said. "So let's take those five minutes now to review Alison's campaign promises."

Pouting angrily, Brittany started to doodle in her notebook.

"Thank you for your cooperation," said Ms. Austin.

Alison turned to look at her friends. Megan grinned widely and Heather gave her the thumbs-up sign.

"Way to go, girlfriend!" Keisha whispered from across the aisle.

Chapter
Three

A SHINING
SURPRISE

s the four girls reached Ellie Goodwin's house on the walk home after school, Alison said, "Let's go up to the attic."

"I wish I could come with you," said Heather. "But I have my ballet lesson."

"It's my afternoon to volunteer at the nursing home," said Keisha.

"And I've got to go to the dentist," said Megan unhappily. "I have to get a cavity filled."

Keisha raised her eyebrows. "Well, that's *guaranteed* to be more fun than some fantastic new adventure."

"*Sure* it is," said Megan, with an exaggerated nod.

Alison hesitated. "Then I guess I'll skip going to the attic," she said. "I was hoping I could go with someone. I'm not in the mood to go alone today."

"Why not give it a try?" said Heather. "Not one of us has ever had a boring trip."

Alison looked thoughtfully at her friends. "Why not?" she said, her eyes suddenly sparkling with anticipation. Waving good-bye, she approached Ellie's front yard. Burgundy roses twined in and out of the white picket fence, contrasting perfectly with the deep pink clusters of peonies that stood guard on either side of the front steps. Hesitating a moment before she opened the gate, Alison took a deep breath. Then she threw her shoulders back and walked up the path to the steps of the white Victorian house.

Standing on the elegant front porch, Alison knocked softly on the door. When there was no answer, she knocked more boldly.

After a few moments, Ellie Goodwin answered the door. Smiling broadly, she leaned down and gave Alison a hug. Then, quickly whispering that she was in the middle of a phone conversation, she told Alison to get the key from the silver box and go on up to the attic if she wished.

Suddenly Ellie's West Highland terrier bounded into the entryway, barking happily when he saw who was there.

"Shhh!" whispered Alison, kneeling on the worn antique oriental carpet. "Where are your manners, Monty? Ellie's on the phone!"

Immediately, the dog rolled over on his back. "Okay, okay," said Alison with a quiet laugh as she scratched his tummy the way he liked. Glancing up, she looked at the gleaming silver box on the small mahogany table. "Gotta go!" she whispered. "The mirror's waiting!"

Carefully holding onto the scrolled golden key, Alison took the steps two at a time, followed closely by Monty. At the top of the stairs, she walked down the hall to the paneled door that was ornamented with a filigreed brass lock plate. Eagerly, Alison turned the key in the lock. As the door opened, she was greeted by the softly pungent scent of cedar as she reached inside and turned on the lights.

"Sit, Monty. Stay," she said. With a sad expression in his eyes, the terrier obediently followed her instructions.

"See you later, alligator," Alison said, before she closed the door behind her.

At the top of the stairs, soft afternoon light filtered through the high dormer windows that graced all four sides of the attic, illuminating the cream, maroon and deep blue shades of the ornate oriental carpet. Across the room, the large steamer trunk waited for her. Smiling, Alison walked up to it, leaned over and grasped the hasp. Then, bending her knees and keeping her back straight as her brother had taught her to do when she lifted something heavy, she raised the lid.

"So what's it going to be today?" Alison asked herself out loud, pretending her friends were still with her. Pulling out an elegant ball gown that belonged in Vienna at the turn of the century, she held the long dress in front of her as she swirled gracefully to imaginary music. "Chamber orchestras and Viennese waltzes? Hardly!" Alison laughed as she placed the gown back into the trunk. "Ball gowns are *definitely* not me."

Closing her eyes, Alison reached deep into the trunk and made a wish. "Bring me something special," she whispered as she pulled out a bundle of white, spangled fabric folded around something heavy.

She shook out the costume.

Kerplunk! A heavy, oddly-shaped case and a curved headpiece fell to the floor. Alison smiled when she opened the case. "Judging from these ice skates," she said, "I'd guess that this white outfit is a skating costume." She paused for a moment, then added in a lower voice, "Brilliant deduction, Sherlock."

She held the costume against her shoulders, then spun around in a circle. Catching a brief glimpse of herself in the mirror, Alison laughed and cried out, "This is great!" She put on the skating outfit, then plopped down on the floor and pulled on the first skate. "Fits perfectly," she said, lacing up one white leather boot, then the other. Before she stood up, Alison reached over and picked up the ruffled white net headpiece and placed it over her blond ponytail.

"I should be able to do this. Ice-skating isn't that different from roller-blading," she said. "Even though skating outdoors in bitter cold weather on a frozen pond was never my favorite thing,

I was okay when I tried it." Continuing her conversation with herself in an effort to keep from feeling too lonely, she said, "Hey, you're the best rollerblader at Lincoln School. You've got the form. And you've got the skill. How hard could it be to ice skate?"

She turned to the mirror. Lifting first one leg, then another, she wobbled for a moment before her body adjusted to the delicate balance that the narrow blades demanded. Once she caught on that the key to this skill was keeping her ankles straight and her body evenly aligned, her confidence increased.

"I can do it," she whispered. "I know I can."

Slowly, carefully, Alison leaned forward, raised her left leg and extended it behind her. With her arms outstretched in a straight line from her shoulders for balance, her back formed a perfect T-shape with her right leg.

She looked happily at the graceful image staring back at her from the mirror. "I've found the balance," she said with a broad smile. "I've found it!"

Whoosh. . . .Whoosh. . . . Alison closed her eyes. Cool air drifted past her face as she skimmed across a smooth surface, her body moving in perfect harmony. Whoosh. . . . Whoosh. . . .

When she opened her eyes, Alison saw her brand new skates cutting perfect figure eights into shining ice.

Chapter
Four

GERMAN LESSONS

Alison discovered she was skating with several other young men and women in an ice rink festooned with flags from around the world. In front of her, a dark-haired young man executed an elegant double axel. His airborne spin looked as effortless as a stroll down the street.

Alison stopped to watch, admiring the young man's artistry. Then she began to glide across the cool, glistening ice. Amazed at her newly discovered skill, after several trips around the crowded rink, she decided to attempt something more challenging.

Turning into position, she pictured every move she was about to make: Gliding backward on the outside of her right blade, Alison leaned into the circle, then pivoted and skated forward briefly before leaping up and turning one and a half times in the air. She landed on the outside of her left blade, then, arms extended, glided backward to continue drawing the circle in the ice.

Looking around to make certain she wouldn't bump into anyone, Alison noticed a girl about her age. She was wearing a red satin skating dress sprinkled with spangles and she looked away as Alison skated gracefully around the rink. Alison smiled as she glided near the girl, but received a cold glare in return.

That girl's about as warm as the ice I'm skating on, Alison thought as she continued her circle. Soon she forgot the chilly girl and was once again caught up in focusing on her own technique.

Amazed that she was so successful on her first attempt at an axel, Alison wondered how she could skate so well. The music from the speakers seemed to guide her, telling her exactly what moves to make. She was even better on ice skates than on in-line skates.

Thrilled that her mind and body could work in such harmony, she watched the girl in red prepare for a spin. Alison memorized every move, especially the way she pulled her arms in tight around her body to increase her speed.

Then, taking her cue from the young woman, Alison prepared to execute a sit spin. Just as she bent her knee, she felt a thump! against her shoulder. Alison was thrown off balance and crashed to the ice. Frowning angrily, Alison watched the young woman in red spangles skate toward the side rail without any apology, where she spoke to an angry-looking man. Just as the girl returned to the ice, Alison stood up and skated toward the center of the rink, ready to try a sit spin one more time. Once again her path was cut off by the girl in red.

Annoyed, Alison stared at her. I can't figure out if she's rude or just lost in concentration, she thought.

"Bitte sagen Sie den Schlittschuhläufern das Eis zu verlassen," a voice suddenly blared over the loudspeaker. "Will all the skaters please clear the ice!" the voice repeated in English. "The preliminary rounds of the World Cup Junior

Ice Skating Championships will begin in five minutes."
Then the speaker made the same announcement in
German, finishing with "... *fängt in fünf Minuten an.*" The
message was repeated two more times in what sounded
to Alison like French and Japanese.

Alison looked about as she stood up. Every sign she
saw was written in German. At least she knew what country
she was in. But how was she to figure out where to go or
what to do? All around the rink, skaters sat in groups
behind a variety of national flags. At the far end, where an

American flag was draped over the rail, several young men and women about her age were gathering. Skating over to the group, Alison stood shyly outside the rail.

"Alison!" said one of the kids. "Thank goodness you're here. We were looking everywhere for you!"

An elegant dark-haired woman in her forties turned to smile at her. The words "Kate Peterson, coach" had been embroidered on the pocket of her red, white, and blue jacket. "We've just been given the order for the elimination rounds," the coach said. "You'll be skating third, behind Etsu Misaka and Katja Kurt."

"Thanks," said Alison, sitting down on the bench so she could adjust the laces on her skates. As she listened quietly, the coach read the order of appearance for the team. Alison's stomach knotted. This competition sounds pretty important, she thought, and it looks like I'm involved. I can't believe I'm doing this. I sure hope I can pull it off.

"*Meine Damen und Herren.*" The words sounded especially important coming out of the loud public address speakers. ". . . Ladies and Gentlemen! Skater number one, representing Japan in the preliminary round of the World Cup Junior Ice Skating Championships: Etsu Misaka!"

Alison leaned forward, clutching the rail as she watched the Japanese teenager glide onto the ice.

The lights faded and Etsu assumed her position to begin the compulsory part of her program. She began by tracing the figure eight three times, first on one foot, then on the other.

"She's good," Alison whispered as she watched Etsu perform the first simple exercise with understated elegance.

"Indeed she is," said Ms. Peterson as they watched Etsu trace her pattern two more times. At the end of the exercise, the only mark Alison saw on the ice was one single figure eight. Etsu had not deviated once from the pattern, the indication of precision and control that judges looked for. "She's even better in the short program and free skating," Ms. Peterson added.

Alison could barely breathe as she watched the Japanese girl complete her routine. The judges awarded Etsu's skill with a 5.5, 5.7 and 5.8 in the three categories.

"That's an excellent score," Ms. Peterson said to Alison. "But you're capable of a better one."

I don't know about that, Alison thought, wondering how she could ever pull this off. What if I mess up? What if I fall on my face in front of all these people?

"Ladies and Gentlemen," blared the loudspeaker. "Representing Germany in the World Cup Junior Championship, Katja Kurt!"

Alison's heart skipped a beat. The spotlight swept in

an arc to the rail, where it shined on the rude young
skater who had looked at her with such hostility and later
crashed into her. As Alison watched, Katja stood perfectly
still, her gaze on the floor. From the other side of the rail,
the man she had spoken to earlier said something brief
to her, then gave her a push onto the ice.

"Did you see that?" said one of the American kids.
"That coach sure doesn't seem very nice."

"Would you believe?" said another. "That coach is her
father."

Alison shook her head. Thank goodness *my* father's
not the coach, she thought.

Spangles sent crimson flashes soaring over the
rink as Katja Kurt moved in and out of the spotlight. She
skated through her first two routines with a tight, forced
smile on her face. The short program and jump-spin
combinations were perfect. By the time she reached the
four-minute free skating program, her smile had relaxed
and she moved into her routine with obvious enjoyment.
Her choreography was creative, and her presentation
was artistic and remarkably original.

Katja is a champion, Alison thought. A real champion.

When Katja finished her three programs, the audience
burst into an extended round of enthusiastic applause.

Suddenly Alison felt as if she had just dropped in

from outer space. How could I have let this happen to me? she asked herself. I'm an impostor, a fake. I'll fall flat on my face when I go out there. I'll humiliate myself in front of ten thousand people.

"I'll never be able to do anything like that," she said.

"Of course you will," said Ms. Peterson. "What happened to that famous can-do attitude of yours?"

"I think it froze to death," she said.

"Nonsense!" said the coach, putting her hand on Alison's shoulder. "You know your routine, and everyone in your category will choose the same compulsory figures. All you have to do is trust yourself and let the music carry you. Just remember to keep your back straight and your chin up on the axel. You're going to be great."

As Alison waited for the judges to tally Katja's scores, the zamboni drove over the ice and smoothed it in preparation for Alison's program.

The loudspeaker announced, ". . . The official scores for Katja Kurt: *fünf Komma acht, fünf Komma neun, fünf Komma sieben . . . cinq point huit, cinq point neuf, cinq point sept . . . go ten hachi, go ten kyu, go ten nana . . .* five point eight, five point nine, five point seven."

After the applause died down, the announcer said, "And now, Ladies and Gentlemen, Alison McCann . . . representing the United States of America!"

Chapter

Five

THE WÜRST CONTEST

he spotlight swept to the American section, dramatically inviting Alison onto the ice.

"Go for it!" Ms. Peterson whispered as she patted Alison on her shoulder. "You can do it!"

Trembling inside, Alison smiled weakly at her coach. I can do it, she repeated in her head. Just follow the music.

She took a deep breath, then glided into the rink to begin the first of the three required figures she had drawn for the Compulsory part of her performance. Thank goodness I have to do these figures in order of difficulty, Alison thought. At least I can start out with the easier stuff.

Slowly, carefully, Alison first traced the figure eight on the clean ice, then skated over the same formation three more times, barely leaving any sign she had made the tracing more than once. Transferring her weight to the other foot, she repeated the process. By the end of the exercise, the figure eight looked like one cleanly drawn design etched into the icy surface of the rink, unbroken by wobbly lines or an uneven angle.

I did it! Alison thought, breathing a quiet sigh of relief before moving into the second and third figures. Although each exercise was more challenging than the last, her confidence increased along with the degree of difficulty.

Before she knew it, Alison moved into the Short Program, a preset routine of jumps, step sequences, spins and step-spin combinations. Knowing she would be judged not only on technical merit, but also on the artistic impression she created, Alison concentrated on the grace of her performance, as well as her form. A big round of applause greeted the end of the program.

Alison nodded to the audience, then focused all her concentration on the Free Skating portion, which would account for fifty percent of her overall score. Closing her eyes, she bowed her head. All right, Alison

McCann, she told herself. Show them what you're made of.

The strains of "Yesterday," the classic Beatles hit, filled the rink. Alison raised her head, allowing the music to tell her what to do. She began by skating in a large circle, picking up speed, visualizing her every move as a perfect companion to the music as it swept her up in its spell. She began with the axel, spinning flawlessly one and a half times in the air and landing on her right foot with perfect grace.

I nailed it! Alison thought. I *can* do it! The music does tell me what to do. I feel totally natural, like I've done this a hundred times before.

Gaining confidence, she moved into the more complicated parts. Her double lutz eased into a double axel–double toe loop combination, fitting together like fluid pieces in a complicated puzzle. As the final strains of the music drew to a close, Alison wanted to yell. She wanted to laugh. She wanted to cry with relief and shout for joy as she bowed her head to the waves of applause that swept her up and carried her back to the American section.

Ms. Peterson beamed. "Beautiful, Alison!"

"You were wonderful!" said several of the other young American skaters, gathering around.

"Thanks," Alison whispered, breathing heavily. "Thanks."

Barely able to speak or catch her breath, time seemed to stop as Alison waited for her scores. Finally, she heard the English words "five point seven, five point eight, five point nine."

"Yesss!" cried Alison as her teammates showered her with hugs.

"Congratulations!" said Ms. Peterson with a wide smile. "That will probably get you into the finals."

Alison fidgeted as she watched the last three skaters. Tugging at her costume, then shifting from skate to skate, she tried to concentrate as the final contestant, a young woman from France, finished her routine.

"I can't believe I'm so nervous!" she whispered.

Ms. Peterson smiled. Without taking her eyes off the skater's last movements, she patted Alison's shoulder and said, "Your division's over now, dear. Why don't you go on back to the dressing room and change clothes?"

In the dressing room, Alison brushed her teeth and splashed cold water on her face, then changed into her sweatsuit. When she returned to the ice rink it was time for the announcement of the finalists. Both she and Katja Kurt had placed in the top seven.

As a special treat for all the skaters, the cup committee had organized a tour of Berlin and the Potsdam Castle. So after the preliminaries were completed, the American team met in the parking lot.

"Here are your van assignments," Ms. Peterson said.

Alison was to ride in the same van with Katja and two other girls, who introduced themselves as Olga Kossmanova, a skater from Russia, and Ellen Baker, an Australian.

Alison followed Ellen and Olga into the van, then turned to Katja.

"Aren't you coming?" Alison asked the German skater.

"I cannot," she said with a polite smile. "I must practice."

Ellen leaned out her window and said, "Oh, please come along with us. We can all use a break."

"That's right, dear," said Ms. Peterson. "It will be good for you."

Hesitating for a moment, Katja nodded and climbed into the van.

"Potsdam Castle is great!" Alison said. "I was never in a castle before."

"I have not before been in a whole castle," said Olga slowly. "I only see . . . ruins . . . and I find the experience excellent."

Ellen laughed. "I, too, have not been in a castle," she said, "And I find it excellent, also."

As the group passed through the grand gates to the van, Ellen asked, "What's next?"

"Where do the kids hang out?" Alison asked, looking straight at Katja. "The movies? the mall?"

"The driver said we will go to the *Wilmersdorfer Straße*."

Alison laughed. "Of course we'll go—if we can ever learn to pronounce it."

"Can we get something to eat there?" Ellen asked.

"Yes," said Katja. "There one finds always food."

Back in the city, the bus drove along the avenue where the most elegant shops in Berlin were located, then past a bombed out cathedral that had been turned into a war memorial.

"The church must have been beautiful. . . ." said Alison.

"It was," Katja said quietly.

They visited the Brandenburg Gate, then strolled along *Wilmersdorfer Straße*. No cars were allowed on the broad avenue, which was filled with shops and street artists. People sold pottery, jewelry, and crafts, while others chalked complicated copies of Renaissance paintings and funny modern cartoons on the sidewalk.

Alison glanced at Katja as she walked down the street, slightly apart from the other three girls. She wondered if the German skater was having any fun. While the other kids laughed and told stories, Katja held back. I feel like I need to learn a special language if I want to communicate with her, Alison thought.

"Umm. What smells so good?" Ellen asked.

Katja finally smiled. "*Würst*," she said, pointing to a food stand covered with an umbrella in the middle of the street. "You are hungry?"

"Starving!" all three kids exclaimed.

"What's *würst*?" Ellen asked.

"It is similar to the American hot dog. There are many kinds," said Katja.

Alison's eyes twinkled. "Let's all see how many different ones we can eat."

"You are serious?" Olga asked as she rubbed her stomach.

"Why not?" Ellen said with a laugh.

"Tasting every kind might be interesting for you," said Katja.

After all the girls had their sandwiches, Alison lifted her *würst* into the air. "Bottoms up!" she said, toasting the others.

"I hope you don't mean that literally," said Ellen, raising her eyebrows and grinning.

Giggling, Olga took a bite of her sausage. "Umm," she said. "Excellent."

By the time the girls ate their *Weißwürst* and *Bratwürst*, they were stuffed.

"I give up! I'll explode if I eat one more bite!" said

Ellen. "You can tell me how the other ones taste."

Alison nodded in agreement.

"We must not stop now," said Olga. "We just begin!"

"You are right," Katja said, then looked directly at Alison. "Are you ready for the *Weinerwürst*?"

If she can do it, I can do it, Alison thought, then nodded.

Smiling brightly, Olga took a small bite of her sandwich. "Delicious," she said.

"Umm," Alison mumbled as she watched Katja gobble down her third *Würst*. Slow down, Ali, she told herself. You don't have to eat faster than Katja, you just have to keep up with how *much* she eats.

After the three girls swallowed their last bite, Katja smiled. "Now for the *Bauernwürst*." Her tone was a clear challenge. "This one is made of ham."

Olga laughed, waving her white napkin in the air as a sign of surrender. "You must continue this big eating without me!" she said.

Alison took a deep breath, then glanced at Katja. "Ready?" she said, trying to convince her stomach to make room for more.

"Yes," said Katja with a curt nod.

I feel almost sick, Alison thought. This is stupid. Why am I stuffing myself? I don't have to beat Katja at everything, do I? She took a bite of her *Bauernwürst*.

Looking at Katja, Alison smiled as graciously as she could. "All right, all right. . . . You win."

Katja took one more tiny bite, then set down her *würst.* "Good," she said with a tight smile. "I cannot make one more swallow!"

The four skaters strolled the avenue, listening to the street music and looking at the art displays. As the sun sank low in the sky, they stopped at a cafe for a cup of cocoa, or *Kakao,* as Katja called it. They couldn't resist sharing a plate of *Apfelstrudel* and *Pflaumenkuchen,* a plum tart, before going to catch the van that would take them back to the stadium.

Pointing toward the end of the block, Katja said, "This is your van."

Alison looked at her. "*Ours?* Aren't you coming with us to the dorm?"

"We'll have a grand time tonight," said Ellen.

Katja stared at the ground. "My papa says I must go home, so I will ride on the bus. I mustn't stay with the others."

"Thank you, for showing us your city," said Olga.

"Yes, thank you," said Ellen, extending her hand to shake Katja's.

Alison smiled. "See you tomorrow," she said.

Chapter Six

GOING
FOR THE
GOLD

zzzzzz. Bzzzzz.

Tossing in her sleep,
Alison tried to keep the noise from a
motorcycle driving on the ice from drowning out all the
music in her dreams. She had just stepped up on the
podium to accept the gold medal.

Bzzzz. Bzzzzzz.

Slowly, Alison realized that the buzzing sound
was her alarm clock. Ugh! She groped for the clock and

pushed in the button. Eyes still closed, she tossed her legs over the side of the bed and sat up.

Ugh! she thought, suddenly coming awake to the present. Today is the championship! Gotta get out on the ice and practice!

Alison jumped into her practice clothes, grabbed her skate case and dashed off to the stadium two blocks away.

The skaters practiced for over two hours that morning. As she worked, Alison tried to visualize herself skating perfectly, imagining how it would feel to win first place. I can win the gold, she told herself over and over, thinking how proud her family and friends would be if she brought home a gold medal. I will win it.

When Katja came toward her, Alison started to wave hello. Her hand stopped in midair. Katja was staring at her, but her face was completely expressionless. Then, without even a nod, she looked away and skimmed past Alison as if they had never met.

Whoa! thought Alison. Every axel and lutz looks fabulous. She's even better than yesterday. And I have to try to beat that! Well, I'm just as tough at competing as Katja is, and I guess I can be just as cold if that's what it takes.

Moving into a sit spin, Alison suddenly teetered, almost losing her balance. So much for sending negative messages to myself, she thought, skating once around the rink to regain her confidence before trying again. Just as Alison eased into position for a second attempt, Katja skated in front of her and, in one simple move, pushed herself into a perfect sit spin. Turning like a human top, she bent one leg and extended the other until she was almost touching the ice.

Alison crashed clumsily to the ground. With her cheeks burning and the sting of the fall working its way right through her tights, she tried to ignore her embarrassment and dismay. I don't know what's worse, she thought with a grim smile: my fanny or my pride.

Without a glance in her direction, Katja glided away. Alison stared after her as she gathered her feet under her. If that's the way you have to play the game, Katja, okay, she thought. I guess we can't even be friendly. Shaking her head, she stood up.

Before Alison finished practicing her routines, the announcer asked the skaters to clear the ice.

Since she wasn't scheduled to compete until after lunch, Alison walked to the cafeteria. Nibbling at a pasta salad that had about as much flavor as sawdust, she looked back on how the German skater had made her lose her composure that morning. Katja is really good at shaking me up, Alison thought. That sure isn't the way I was taught to compete. She couldn't intimidate me, though, if I didn't allow it. I've got to concentrate on that gold medal, not Katja Kurt. I'll win the way I always have—by just doing my best.

She returned to the arena and sat next to Ms. Peterson. Throughout the afternoon, she tried to absorb the best from each skater who entered the rink. Glancing around the arena, she caught a glimpse of Katja.

In their age category, Katja drew last place and Etsu Misaka competed third, just before Alison. As Alison watched the Japanese skater, she could see determination and grit written on her face, but nothing mean. Nothing mean or ugly at all.

Etsu's scores put her in first place.

"You're on, Alison," said Ms. Peterson softly. "Go for the gold and knock their socks off!"

The spotlight swept to the American bench, and Alison stood up to take her turn. Even though she barely saw the crowd and her palms were damp, as she glided into her starting position she smiled broadly around the arena.

Tracing and retracing the figures in the Compulsory, she glided into the rhythm of her routine. She felt as if she'd been ice skating since the day she was born.

Only four minutes to go, Alison told herself as she

began the Free Skating portion. Halfway through her program, she picked up speed for the double lutz.

The moment her body lifted into the air, Alison sensed her lack of balance. She was tilted! With a wobbly thud, she landed unsteadily on her left foot, almost falling to her knees.

That was close, she thought as she went on with her routine. And it will cost me points, too.

Alison tried to hide her disappointment behind a confident smile as she made her closing bow. After the applause died down, she waited anxiously to hear her scores. Finally the loudspeakers announced she had gotten 5.8, 5.9, 5.7..

Considering my slip up, that's good, she thought. So far, it's first place.

Katja was the final skater in the competition. When her turn came, Alison was still in first place. She fought to remain calm as she watched. In the Free Skating, Katja's final event, every spin was superb, every leap was perfect. There goes my gold, Alison thought sadly, visualizing the first-place medal being lifted from around her neck.

Then suddenly, in an attempt at a triple lutz, Katja crashed onto the ice.

Oh no! Alison thought. . . . Oh yes. The gold medal's mine for sure! She stared into the rink, ashamed that

even though Katja might be hurt, she was hoping the fall would leave her an opening for the top prize.

Katja's hands barely touched the ice before she stood up and sped away, only skipping a beat or two in her routine. Moments before the uplifting violin music came to a close, an expression of sudden determination appeared on her face.

She skated in a wide circle to build up momentum, the muscles of her powerful legs rippling. Then her body lifted into the air. Katja executed a flawless double toe loop–triple toe loop combination. It was the most perfect move Alison could imagine.

In an instant, every person in the stadium was standing. Applause, whistles, and cheers rocked the rink.

"Extraordinary courage," said Ms. Peterson. "To come back from a bad fall and execute a combination like that . . . I've never seen anything like it."

The applause seemed to last forever. The wait for the scores lasted even longer.

At last the loudspeaker announced: "Five point nine, six point zero, five point nine."

"Extraordinary," repeated Ms. Peterson with awe. "Getting a six-oh after a fall is unheard of. She's being rewarded not

only for her talent, but for risk taking and courage."

Alison stared at the floor. I should be thrilled with second place, she told herself. A silver medal is good. Very good. She felt Ms. Peterson's comforting hand on her shoulder.

Across the rink, Coach Kurt was shaking a finger at Katja. She stood erect, her head high, her jaws set, her arms hanging stiffly at her sides. Her face looked as if it had been carved in stone.

When the winners were called, Alison walked with Katja and a French girl to the center of the arena. As second-place winner, she stood one step below Katja. After the German national anthem faded away, the judge hung a shiny silver medal around Alison's neck. Smiling, she stood proudly as she sang "The Star Spangled Banner."

At the end of the awards ceremony, Alison took a deep breath and then turned to Katja. "Congratulations," she said. "You deserve to win."

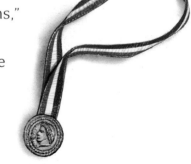

Katja's face broke into a wide smile. "Thank you," she said.

Chapter
Seven

A TWO-TIME
LOSER?

As darkness fell, Alison looked around the empty skating stadium, trying to memorize every last detail. Then she walked slowly to the locker room and stood in front of the mirror.

"It's time to go," she said to her image. Alison swallowed as she smoothed her silky blond hair. Then she closed her eyes.

When she opened them, she was standing in Ellie Goodwin's attic. After admiring the white net and silver spangles one last time, she packed the skating outfit away, then sat quietly for a moment. The late afternoon light, shining brightly through the dormer windows, cast a golden glow onto the brass fittings of the old fashioned trunk as she closed the lid.

"Okay, Ali," said Heather when the Magic Attic Club met Saturday afternoon. "Tell us everything about it."

The Four Musketeers sat on the fuzzy white rug in Heather's bedroom. Leaning into the circle, Alison smiled. "Well," she said. "Can you imagine me as a champion ice skater?"

"Definitely," said Megan.

"Of course," said Keisha.

When Alison had finished, Megan said, "It seems like competition is a serious part of your life these days."

Alison nodded. "You're right," she said. "And there are all kinds of competitions—and competitors. I just hope the election turns out better than the skating competition."

With a quick intake of breath, Heather asked, "How are you going to feel if you lose the election to Brittany?"

Alison thought for a moment. "Rotten," she said.

"Hey," said Keisha. "Stay cool. You're going to win."

Alison shrugged. "I hope you're right," she said. "But if I don't, at least I'll know I played fair and tried my best."

When the girls arrived at school Monday morning, they were greeted by an unnaturally cheerful Brittany.

"Hi, girls. Hi, Alison."

Alison nodded, then said, "No matter how the election turns out, Brittany, I hope there will be no hard feelings between us."

Brittany's smile looked forced. "Of course," she said, then without another word, turned her back on the four friends.

As soon as the class quieted down, Ms. Austin

handed a ballot to each student. "After you've voted," she said, "fold your ballot in half. Bring it to my desk and put it through the slot on top of the box."

The moment she finished speaking, Brittany's hand shot up. "When will you count the votes?"

"The winners will be announced at the all-school assembly this afternoon."

Alison stared at the ballot on her desk, reading Brittany's and her name over and over. I feel like it's awfully stuck up to vote for myself, she thought. But, she added with a secret smile, I'd feel even worse if I helped elect Brittany. She wouldn't even think of voting for *her* opponent.

That afternoon the students assembled in the auditorium. The candidates for president, vice president, secretary and treasurer for every grade stood in groups on the stage.

Grade by grade, Mr. Roberts, the school principal, announced the results of the class elections.

"The president of the first grade is Alexander Munzinger. The vice president is . . ."

This is going to take *forever*, Alison thought, shifting from one foot to another. Maybe he'll get to us by the time I count to a hundred. One, two, three . . .

. . . Seventy-eight, seventy-nine, eighty.

"And the third grade secretary . . ."

Brittany's nervous, too, Alison thought. She can't stop jiggling her leg. A hundred and one, a hundred and two, a hundred and three.

"Now let's see. The president of the fifth-grade class is . . ."

This was it! Alison crossed her fingers. Mr. Roberts fumbled with his paper. Come on, Mr. R.!

". . .The president is Alison McCann."

I did it! thought Alison, breaking into a wide grin. I did it.

As soon as the assembly ended, Alison hurried to her classroom. She was greeted by cheers the moment she walked in the door. Alison waved both hands in the air and smiled at her friends.

"Speech!" cried Matt Van Horn.

"Speech!" echoed Heather, Keisha, and Megan.

Ms. Austin looked at Alison and said, "Congratulations, Alison."

"Thank you," said Alison. "I'm glad I didn't give up."

"Why don't you come say a few words to the class?" said Ms. Austin.

As Alison walked to the front of the room, she didn't have the slightest notion of what she was going to say until she started to speak.

"Thank you for your votes, everybody," she said, then waited for the applause to die down before she continued. "In the past few days, I've been thinking a lot about winning."

"You could have fooled us," Ben called out.

After the kids stopped laughing, Alison added, "Well, trust me, I've thought a lot about losing, too. Goodness knows," she glanced at her Magic Attic Club friends, then at Brittany, "I certainly understand what *that* feels like."

"I don't know how good I'll be at this job. But I do know that I'll work hard for you and give it everything I've got. I promise I'll try to be the best fifth-grade president Lincoln has ever had." She paused for a moment. "I also promise I'll find out what the mystery meat in the cafeteria is made of."

The class broke into cheers as Alison headed to her seat.

Diary

Dear Diary,

You wouldn't believe what happened to me! I won the silver medal in the World Cup Junior Ice Skating Championship!

I have so many things to tell you that my thoughts are all jumbled up. I wish I could sort everything out real easily, but so much happened last week that sad and happy are mixed together in my head

For instance, thinking about how much fun I had competing in the Junior Ice Skating Championships makes me happy. Speaking of fun, though, I don't think Katja will ever have any until her father eases up on her. And it sure doesn't look like that's going to happen anytime soon! I feel so sorry for her!

As for me being the new president of the

class, that makes me nervous and excited and super happy! The night of the election, Mom and Dad took me and the boys, along with Heather and Megan and Keisha, out to celebrate. My best friends just had to come along I couldn't have won without their help. They were absolutely fabulous!

Well, on to the best part of all. I couldn't exactly tell anybody but you, Diary, but I'm pretty proud of myself for being elected class president. To be honest, I really think it's cool. I worked hard and I won fair and square. I was so disappointed that I didn't win the gold medal for ice skating, but the election made up for it. And it was a landslide! It looks like I won the gold medal, after all. It just wasn't the way I expected

That's all for now.

Love, Me. Alison